CONTENTS

Stories retold by Maureen Spurgeon

First published 1995 by Brown Watson
The Old Mill, 76 Fleckney Road,
Kibworth Beauchamp,
Leicestershire, England

Reprinted 1996, 1997, 1999, 2000, 2001, 2003, 2005

ISBN: 0-7097-1024 -0
©1995 Brown Watson, England

Printed in China

FAIRY TALE
TREASURY

BOOK TWO

Brown Watson
ENGLAND

Alice in Wonderland

Alice was tired of sitting on the bank and having nothing much to do. The sun made her feel sleepy, and she was just wondering about making a daisy chain – when a white rabbit ran past saying, "Oh, dear! Oh, dear! I shall be too late!" and taking a watch from his waistcoat pocket!

Alice had never seen a white rabbit with a waistcoat, or a pocket watch, so she followed him to see where he was going. And when the White Rabbit went down a rabbit hole – down went Alice after it.

Suddenly, Alice felt herself falling. She landed on a heap of dry leaves. "Oh dear," she heard the White Rabbit saying, "how late it is getting!"

All at once, he vanished from sight – leaving Alice in a long, low hall with locked doors all around. Alice came across a little table on which there was a key. But, which door did it fit?

Then she came across a tiny door behind a curtain. She turned the key in the lock, and the door opened. Kneeling down, she could see a beautiful garden, with bright flower beds and water fountains.

"Now," thought Alice, "how do I get out?" On the table where the key had been, there was a bottle with "DRINK ME!" written on a label around the neck – the most delicious drink Alice had ever tasted!

And with every drop, Alice
became smaller and smaller –
until she was just the right size to
get through the little door and
into the beautiful garden. If only
she had not left the key on the
table . . .

Then, she found a box with a cake inside. In currants were the words, "EAT ME." So, Alice did, growing taller and taller – until she was much too big to go through the door, even though she had the key!

Alice was so sad, she began to cry. Before long, there was the patter of feet and in came the White Rabbit. The sight of such a big, tall Alice frightened him so much, he dropped the fan and gloves he was carrying.

Alice picked up the fan, quickly dropping it when she found herself shrinking again! Her foot slipped, and – splash! She was up to her chin in the pool of tears she had wept when she had been so big and tall.

In the pool of tears was also a
duck, a dodo – and a mouse who
told a story to get everyone dry!
"Mary Ann!" called a voice.
"Fetch me my gloves this minute!"
It was the   White Rabbit.

This time, Alice followed him to a little house with "W. RABBIT" on the door. Coming out the other side, she saw a huge mushroom, about as tall as she was now, on which a caterpillar sat, smoking a pipe!

The caterpillar said that eating
one side of the mushroom would
make her taller, the other side
smaller. So Alice took a piece of
each. A Cheshire Cat grinned at
her from a tree.

"Please," said Alice to the cat, "which way should I go?"

"That way," said the cat waving his right paw, "lives the Mad Hatter, and that way," waving his other paw, "lives the March Hare!"

The March Hare's house had a roof thatched with fur and chimneys shaped like long ears! He and the Mad Hatter sat outside at a table, resting their elbows on a very sleepy little dormouse.

"Tell us a story!" ordered the
March Hare.

"Well," said Alice, taken by
surprise, "I don't think . . ."

"Don't think?" he echoed. "Then
you shouldn't talk!"

That was enough to make Alice
march away from the table. Quite
by chance she saw one of the
trees had a door set in it. When
Alice opened it, she was in the
hall again.

Nibbling one piece of the caterpillar's mushroom, then the other, Alice made herself the right size to get the key then go through the little door and out into the beautiful garden, at last!

Here, two gardeners were painting white roses red! "We planted a white rose by mistake!" explained one, "and if the queen finds out . . . . Oh no! Here she comes now!"

The Queen of Hearts stopped
when she saw Alice. "What is
your name, child?" she asked.
"My name," said Alice, "is Alice."
"Can you play croquet?"
"Oh, yes!" cried Alice.

Alice had never played croquet using flamingoes to hit curled-up hedgehogs! Before long the game was a real mess, with the queen yelling "Off with his head!" every other minute.

Suddenly, the cry went up, "The trial is beginning!"

"What trial?" asked Alice – but everyone was already running ahead, carrying her along with them into a big court room.

"The charge is," said the White
Rabbit, "that the Knave of Hearts
stole some tarts!"
"Call the first witness!" said the
king. And to her great surprise,
the White Rabbit called, "Alice!"

"What do you know of this?" asked the king.

"Nothing whatsoever," said Alice.

"Off with her head!" shouted the Queen of Hearts, red in the face.

"You?" went on Alice. "You're only a pack of cards!"

At once, the cards rose up and came flying down on her! Alice gave a little scream – and found herself back on the bank.
Her adventures in Wonderland had only been a wonderful dream!

Sleeping Beauty

THERE was once a king and queen who seemed to have everything that anyone could possibly want. They had a lovely palace, huge estates, and all the people in the kingdom loved them. Yet, still they longed for just one thing more – a child of their own.

39

Then, after many a sad and lonely year, a baby daughter was born.

The king and queen were so happy.

"We shall give a party to celebrate," announced the king.

"And all the fairies shall be invited!" cried the queen.

So the invitations were written, ready for birds to take them to all parts of the kingdom. Nobody saw one invitation fluttering down into the lake . . .

It was the invitation for the Fairy Carabos.

When she heard there was to be a royal party, and she was not invited, she was furious!

She ran to the palace, where
the other fairies were gathered
around the cradle, ready to bless
the royal baby with gifts of
kindness, happiness and beauty.

"Hah!" screamed a cruel, mocking voice. "Heed the spell of Carabos! On her fifteenth birthday, the princess will prick her finger on a spindle, and die!"

With a wild cackle of laughter
which rang all round the palace,
Carabos swept out, nodding her
head in satisfaction to hear the
gasps of horror behind her.

The fairies knew Carabos was far more powerful than them.

"But, perhaps," one said at last, "we can put our magic together and change the spell, just a little ..."

"It means the princess will sleep for a hundred years when she pricks her finger," she told the king and queen. "But at least she will not die."

"All the spindles in the kingdom
must be broken!" cried the king.
"Then our child will be safe!"

Soon, the evil spell was forgotten. The princess grew beautiful, often dreaming of the handsome prince she hoped to marry, one day.

As the day of her fifteenth birthday approached, the king and queen planned the most splendid party. All the servants were very busy.

So the princess was left alone to wander through the grounds by herself. And that is how she came across a little door she had never seen before . . .

Soon, the princess was climbing a staircase which led to the very top of a high tower. There sat an old woman at a spinning wheel — something completely new to her . . .

"Come, learn to spin, my dear," cackled the old woman. "Just take the spindle . . ."

And in one terrible instant, the wicked spell of Carabos came true!

The beautiful young princess pricked her finger and fell to the ground. And even the wild screams of laughter from Carabos faded into complete silence.

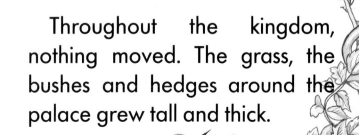

Throughout the kingdom, nothing moved. The grass, the bushes and hedges around the palace grew tall and thick.

The story of the Sleeping Beauty became a legend, a tale which parents told their children. Until, one day, a brave prince decided to try and discover the truth . . .

On and on he rode, until he came to the forest, so thick and dark, there seemed no way in. But, as he raised his sword to cut through the greenery, a strange thing happened . . .

The forest of trees and bushes parted, so that he could lead his horse to the palace! Nothing had changed since the day when the evil spell of Carabos had come true . . .

The prince went through the little door and climbed the stairs. The last thing he expected to see was the princess, still young, still fast asleep . . .

She was so lovely, the prince fell in love with her at once. As he bent to kiss her, she opened her eyes and gave him a sweet smile.

At the same moment, the birds outside the window began singing, the leaves rustled in the breeze, and a bell sounded in the kitchen. The long sleep was over!

The prince had shown that love and courage could triumph over the worst evil! And the princess? She knew he was the sweetheart she had always dreamed of marrying, one day.

Cinderella

Once, Cinderella and her father, the Baron, had lived alone, after the death of her mother when she was a baby. She loved him dearly.

How she sighed, remembering those happy days before her father married a widow with two daughters of her own.

The widow's daughters were so ugly and cruel, they quickly became known as The Ugly Sisters.

Soon, the Baron's daughter was made to do all the housework.

She was dressed in rags, and because she spent so much time in the kitchen among the cinders, they called her "Cinderella".

Then, one morning, Cinderella heard a loud knock at the door.

It was a message from the royal palace, sent to all the houses in the kingdom.

"Invitations to a Grand Ball in honour of the Prince Charming" squealed the Ugly Sisters.

Cinderella's heart began to beat.

She ran up the cellar steps, almost bumping into the Baron!

"Father!" she panted, "the invitations that have come for the Grand Ball! I can go, can't I?"

But before the Baron could answer, Cinderella's step-mother shouted out:

"You? Go to the Ball dressed in your rags? Talk sense, Cinderella! You're only fit to stay at home!"

Cinderella knew the Baron was too afraid of his wife to say anything. The Ugly Sisters were delighted, glad of an excuse to make Cinderella work harder than ever.

"Alter my dress!" "Brush my hair!" "Shine my shoes!" "Iron my gloves!"

They meant to look their very best for the handsome Prince Charming.

By the evening of the Ball, Cinderella was so unhappy she could hardly bear it. Alone in the house, she sat by the fire, her tears falling into the cold, black cinders.

Then, a dazzling glow of light seemed to fill the kitchen, making it bright and warm.

"Do not cry, Cinderella", came a soft voice. "I am here to help you."

"H — help me?" Cinderella stammered. "But, how? Who — who are you?"

"Your Fairy Godmother," came the reply. "And with my magic wand, I shall see that you go to the Ball!"

Before Cinderella could answer, her Fairy Godmother gave a tap with her wand — and, in an instant, her rags became the most beautiful ball gown she could ever have imagined!

"I shall need a pumpkin . . ." said
the Fairy Godmother.

"There's one in the kitchen
garden . . ." said Cinderella.

The Fairy Godmother turned a fat pumpkin into a crystal coach! Four mice became white ponies, and two rats were changed into footmen!

"Thank you, Fairy Godmother!" cried Cinderella.

"Just remember my magic can only last until midnight!" her Godmother smiled.

Well, what a stir when Cinderella arrived at the Palace! Everyone wanted to know who the beautiful young girl was — including Prince Charming, who at once came up to her.

They danced the whole evening, falling in love with each hour that slipped by.

The Ugly Sisters had no idea that the beautiful girl was Cinderella!

On the first stroke of midnight, Cinderella remembered what her Fairy Godmother had said.

"I — I have to go!" she cried, and turned to run down the stairs.

Prince Charming was surprised and knew he had to see the beautiful girl again.

The only clue she left was a tiny, glass slipper . . .

There was great excitement next day. A royal procession came around all the streets, with a page carrying the glass slipper on a red cushion.

"Whoever this slipper fits," said the Royal Herald, "shall marry Prince Charming!"

"It will fit me!" squealed the first Ugly Sister. "It will fit me!"

"No, me!" screamed her sister.

But, the slipper was much too small for either of them.

"But, this is the last house!" cried the Herald. "Is there nobody else?"

"Only my daughter," said the Baron quickly. "I'll call her."

And even before he put the slipper on Cinderella's tiny foot, the Prince knew she was the girl he loved.

Soon, Cinderella and the Prince celebrated their marriage. And somewhere, Cinderella knew, her Fairy Godmother was there, smiling.

Stories I have read

Goldilocks and the Three Bears ☐

Red Riding Hood ☐

Snow White and the Seven Dwarfs ☐

The Ugly Duckling ☐

The Wizard of Oz ☐

Pinocchio ☐